I am a bug.

jug

Hug a Bug

Consultants

Ashley Bishop, Ed.D.
Sue Bishop, M.E.D.

Publishing Credits

Dona Herweck Rice, *Editor-in-Chief*
Robin Erickson, *Production Director*
Lee Aucoin, *Creative Director*
Tim J. Bradley, *Illustrator Manager*
Jason Peltz, *Illustrator*
Sharon Coan, *Project Manager*
Jamey Acosta, *Editor*
Rachelle Cracchiolo, M.A.Ed., *Publisher*

Teacher Created Materials
5301 Oceanus Drive
Huntington Beach, CA 92649-1030
http://www.tcmpub.com

ISBN 978-1-4333-2937-1

bug

I am in a jug.

mug

This is my mug.

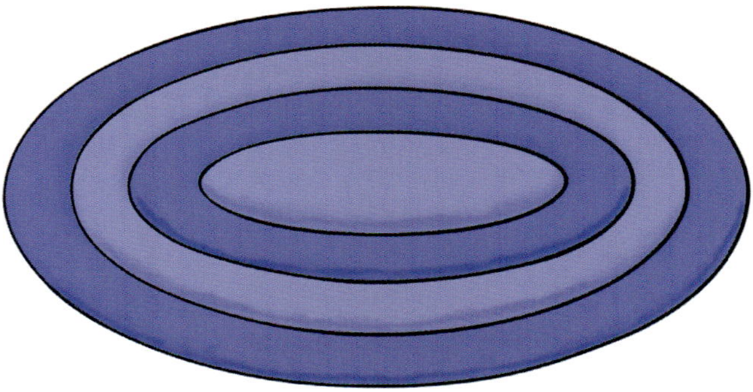

rug

This is my rug.

I like hugs!

Glossary

 bug	 hugs
 jug	 mug
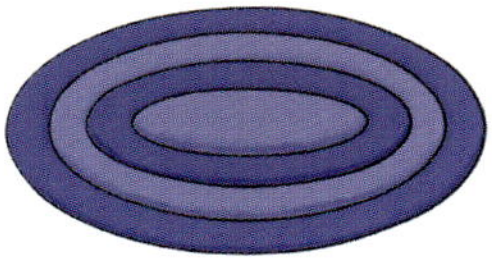 rug	**Sight Words** I am a in This is my like

Extension Activities

Read the story together with your child. Use the discussion questions before, during, and after your reading to deepen your child's understanding of the story and the rime (word family) that is introduced.

The activities provide fun ideas for continuing the conversation about the story and the vocabulary that is introduced. They will help your child make personal connections to the story and use the vocabulary to describe prior experiences.

Discussion Questions

- Why would a bug be in a jug?
- Can a bug drink from a mug? Who drinks out of a mug?
- Do you like hugs? Who do you like to hug?

Activities at Home

- Look in your garden for different kinds of bugs. Have your child draw a picture of a bug.
- Make a list of as many *-ug* words as you can with your child. Have your child write a sentence using an *-ug* word.